SOME PETS

PET SHOW TODAY!

words by
ANGELA DiTERLIZZI

pets by
BRENDAN WENZEL

SOME
PETS

BEACH LANE BOOKS
New York   London
Toronto   Sydney   New Delhi

Some pets
SIT.

Some pets
STAY.

Some pets
FETCH.

And some pets
PLAY!

Some pets
SLITHER.

Some pets
BOUND.

Some pets
SCURRY
round and round.

Some pets
SQUEAL.

Some pets
SQUAWK.

Some pets
SQUEAK.

And
some pets
TALK.

Some pets
PECK.

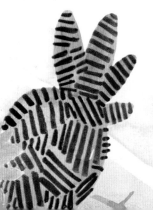

Some pets
NIBBLE.

Some pets
DROOL
on their kibble!

Some pets
SQUEEZE.

Some pets
NUZZLE.

Some pets
LICK.

Some pets
CUDDLE.

Whether
FLUFFY, FEATHERED,
CRAWLY, CUTE,
SILLY, STRANGE,
SCALY, BRUTE,
BIG or SMALL,

or a
BLEND—

SOME PETS
can be . . .

someone's
BEST FRIEND!

WHAT'S THAT PET ?!

MR. SQUEEZE
THE CHAMELEON

ROCK PIGEON
(IS NOT A PET)

SKY
THE GREAT DANE

CORA
THE BULLDOG

MAVIS
THE POODLE

DROOPS
THE BEAGLE

PANCAKES
THE GOLDEN RETRIEVER

LUCY
THE CHIHUAHUA

HAZELNUT
THE POMERANIAN

MIMI
THE MUTT

SLEDGEHAMSTER
THE HAMSTER

SCAMP
THE YORKSHIRE TERRIER

SIR WINSTON
THE PUG

VITTLES
THE CHINCHILLA

SQUIRREL
(ALSO NOT A PET)

PICKLES
THE PARAKEET

SCREAMIN' GENE
THE MACAW

DRAGON
THE IGUANA

COXSACKIE
THE COCKATOO

KOKONUT
THE HORSE

JEFF
THE HEDGEHOG

RUPERT
THE CORN SNAKE

AUGUSTUS
THE POT-BELLIED PIG

OSKAR
THE BRITISH SHORTHAIR

GUILLERMO
THE GUINEA PIG

CLUCKERS
THE CHICKEN

SMOKEY
THE TUXEDO

NORM
THE TABBY

MURF
THE SIAMESE

LEMON DROPS
THE EXOTIC SHORTHAIR

BLASTOFF
THE FANCY MOUSE

PHILLIP
THE DUTCH RABBIT

EVIE
THE PYGMY GOAT